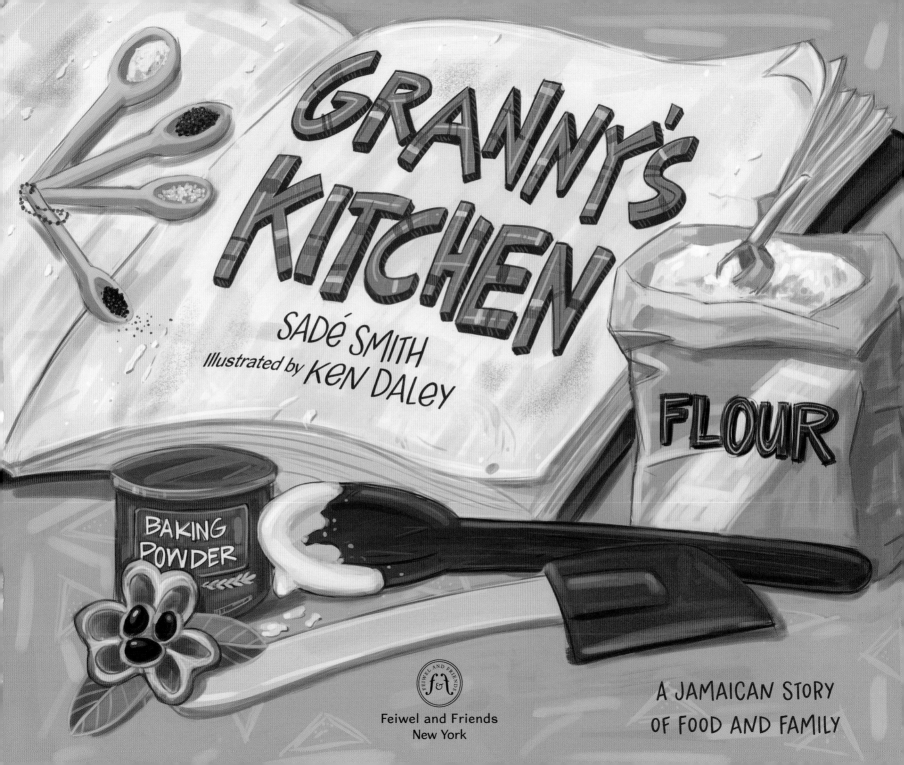

# GRANNY'S KITCHEN

SADé SMITH

Illustrated by KEN DALEY

FLOUR

BAKING POWDER

Feiwel and Friends
New York

A JAMAICAN STORY
OF FOOD AND FAMILY

A Feiwel and Friends Book
An imprint of Macmillan Publishing Group, LLC
120 Broadway, New York, NY 10271
mackids.com

Library of Congress Cataloging-in-Publication Data is available.

First edition, 2022
Book design by Cindy De La Cruz
Art rendered in Photoshop.
Feiwel and Friends logo designed by Filomena Tuosto
Printed in China by RR Donnelley Asia Printing Solutions
Ltd., Dongguan City, Guangdong Province

ISBN 978-1-250-80633-8  (hardcover)
10  9  8  7  6  5  4  3  2  1

*For my Grandmother Curline
and my sister Sushannah*
—S.S.

*To my beloved grandmas:
Ulie, Thomasine, and Ivy*
—K.D.

**SHELLY-ANN LIVED** on the beautiful island of Jamaica, where the sun is always shining and the weather is sweet.

Her grandmother had a lot of vegetables and fruit trees growing in her yard and all around her house.

She even had a big mango tree! Shelly-Ann liked to climb it, or lie under it, snacking on mangoes all day long.

Shelly-Ann loved when her grandmother took her to the market to buy rice, which she would sometimes carry on top of her head. That always made Shelly-Ann laugh. Shelly-Ann loved her grandmother. In fact, Granny was Shelly-Ann's most favorite person in the whole wide world.

One afternoon, Shelly-Ann was picking vegetables in the garden when the scent of sweet peppers made her *very* hungry, so she went into the house to ask her grandmother for something to eat.

"Granny, how do you make dumplins?" Shelly-Ann asked.

Granny smiled and said, "GYAL, YOU BETTA CAN COOK!" And she promised to teach her.

Granny pulled out her iron pot and recited the recipe to Shelly-Ann from memory. "Knead two cups of flour with three-quarters of a cup of water," said Granny. "And don't forget the pinch of salt!"

Shelly-Ann rushed to the pantry to get the flour. Her mouth watered as she imagined taking a bite of a soft, fluffy dumplin.

FLOUR

BAKING POWDER

But when she took them out of the frying pan, they were all black and burnt.

"I can't cook!" cried Shelly-Ann.

"Don't worry," said Granny. "Dumplins burn easily if you leave them in the frying pan for too long. You will get it right next time."

The next day, Shelly-Ann was playing hopscotch on the sidewalk when she became hungry.

GRRROOOWWWL!

So she went inside and asked her grandmother for something to eat. "Granny, how do you make ackee?" Granny replied, "GYAL, YOU BETTA CAN COOK!"

ACKEE

Ingredients:
1 onion
1 Bell pepper
1 Tomato
1 Sprig of thyme
1 Scotch bonnet pepper
1 pinch of salt
1 tsp Black pepper
1 ripe ackee
¼ cup of oil

Directions:
Pick a ripe ackee that has split open on its own. Peel only the yellow ~~~ ackee and boil ~~~ in water until tender, th~~~ fry until cooked through. Make su~~~ DO NOT EVER eat the se~~~

Luckily, Shelly-Ann could *just* reach the bright orange fruit on the tree in Granny's backyard . . . with a little help!

Granny pulled out her recipe card and read the instructions to Shelly-Ann. "Pick a ripe ackee that has split open on its own. Peel the ackee and boil only the yellow parts in water until tender, then fry until cooked through. Make sure you DO NOT EVER eat the seeds!"

The yellow ackee swirled around the pot until it was soft and tender.
When Shelly-Ann was finished frying it, she thought the ackee looked a bit like scrambled eggs. But when she took a bite, the ackee was too soft.
"I can't cook!" cried Shelly-Ann.
"Don't worry," said Granny.
"Ackee is easy to overcook.
You will get it right next time."

A few days later, Shelly-Ann was skipping rope on the porch when her stomach rumbled, so she went to ask her grandmother for something to eat. "Granny, how do you make saltfish?" Granny smiled and answered, "GYAL, YOU BETTA CAN COOK!"

Granny went to the cupboard to pull out a skillet and to gather the ingredients.
"Soak the cod fish in water for two hours and then sauté all your vegetables and herbs.
Add the saltfish, mix it all together, and cook until tender."

The scent of spices filled the entire kitchen.
Shelly-Ann was so excited to try the fish.
But when she took a bite, it was too salty.
"I can't cook!" cried Shelly-Ann.
"Don't worry, you will get it right next time,"
said Granny. "The fish needs to soak a long
time to make it less salty."

The following morning, Shelly-Ann was chasing chickens around the coop. It made her very hungry, so once again, she went inside to ask her grandmother for something to eat.

"Granny, how do you make plantains?"

Granny grinned.

"I know, I know," Shelly-Ann said with a giggle. "GYAL, YOU BETTA CAN COOK!"

Granny laughed as she pulled out a frying pan and a spatula.
"Pick some ripe plantains, then peel and slice them into thin pieces.
Fry the plantain slices in oil until brown and tender," Granny told Shelly-Ann.

The slices of plantain popped and sizzled in the oil, and Shelly-Ann's mouth watered. But when she took a bite, they were too mushy.

"I can't cook!" cried Shelly-Ann.

"Plantain slices need to be a little bit thinner," said Granny. "Don't worry, you will get it right next time."

"I don't want to learn how to cook anymore," Shelly-Ann said. "I've tried and tried, and I *never* get it right."

Granny wiped Shelly-Ann's tears, then picked up her homemade recipe book and handed it to her granddaughter. "If you try and don't succeed, try, try, and try again."

When Shelly-Ann woke up the next morning, she noticed that Granny was still asleep.
She was very hungry, so she tiptoed into Granny's bedroom.
"Granny," whispered Shelly-Ann, "can you make me something good for breakfast?"
With a sigh, Granny replied, "I am too tired to cook this morning."
And she closed her eyes and went back to sleep.

Shelly-Ann went to the kitchen table and sat down. She opened the recipe book to find old pictures of family and friends from the neighborhood enjoying Granny's prize-winning dumplins. The smiles on all their faces reminded Shelly-Ann how much joy Granny's dumplins bring to everyone.

"It must have taken Granny a lot of practice to make the perfect dumplins," Shelly-Ann said to herself.

Then she became excited. "I just have to try, try, and try again," Shelly-Ann said. "And don't forget the pinch of salt!"

DUMPLIN' RECIPE

Ingredients:

2 cups of flour
3/4 cup of water
1/2 tsp of salt
3 tsp of Baking powder
1/2 cup of oil

She went out to the yard to gather what she needed. She hauled all the ingredients into the kitchen and pulled out a big Dutch pot and a skillet from the cupboard.

She fried the dumplins.
She cooked the ackee.
She soaked the saltfish.
She sliced the plantain.
Just like Granny had taught her.

Shelly-Ann put all of the food onto two
big plates and tiptoed into Granny's room.

Granny opened her eyes.
"Dumplins? Ackee? Saltfish? *And* plantains?"
Granny was delighted.

Granny took one bite of the food.

Then she took another.

And another.

"GYAL, YOU CAN COOK!" Granny exclaimed.
Shelly-Ann beamed with joy. "I can?"
Granny nodded and said, "And it's even
better because you made it with love."

Shelly-Ann was very proud of herself for making Granny the perfect breakfast.

The dumplins were not burnt . . . well, maybe a little.

The ackee was not too soft . . . most of it, anyway.

The saltfish was not too salty . . . nothing a little pepper couldn't fix.

And the plantains were not too mushy . . . at least the ones in the back weren't.

Everything was irie.

# GRANNY'S RECIPES

(Please have an adult present when cooking and following recipes.)

## Fried or Boiled Dumplings (Dumplins)

**Ingredients:**
2 cups flour
3 teaspoons baking powder (for fried dumplings only)
1/2 teaspoon salt
3/4 cup water
1/2 cup vegetable oil (for fried dumplings only)

**For fried dumplings:** Mix flour, baking powder, and salt in a large mixing bowl. Add water little by little to create a doughy mixture. (Note: You may not need all the water. If dough becomes too wet, add a little bit more flour. Dough should be a bit sticky but not runny.) Knead dough until it is consistent. Set aside for 10–15 minutes. Pour cooking oil into a large frying pan and set the stove to medium-high heat. Roll small pieces of dough into balls (slightly bigger than a golf ball) and place into the hot oil in the frying pan. Be sure to periodically turn dumplings over when they turn brown. Cook until fluffy and brown on all sides, approximately 5–7 minutes. Remove dumplings from pan and place on a paper towel to absorb excess oil.

Enjoy and eat when cool!

**For boiled dumplings:** Make the dough as you would for fried dumplings, but do not add baking powder. After the dough has rested for 10–15 minutes, roll small pieces of dough into balls (slightly bigger than a golf ball) and lightly press your thumb into the middle of the dough to create a shallow dimple. You may also roll the dough into small finger shapes called "spinnas" to create a different shape of dumpling. Add the dough to a pot of soup and boil. Dumplings will cook in approximately 20 minutes but should be left in the soup until the soup is finished cooking.

Enjoy!
Servings: 8–10 dumplings

## Ackee

**Ingredients:**
1/4 cup vegetable oil
1 onion, chopped
1 bell pepper, chopped
1 tomato, diced
2 sprigs fresh thyme, chopped in half
1 Scotch bonnet pepper, chopped (optional)
1 (19-ounce) can ackee
1 pinch salt
1 teaspoon black pepper

**Directions:**
Heat oil in a large skillet or frying pan over medium-high heat. Sauté onion and bell pepper until onions become translucent. Add in tomato, thyme, and Scotch bonnet pepper and stir until cooked, approximately 30–45 seconds. Drain the canned ackee and rinse it in water and drain again. Add ackee to sautéed vegetable mixture and stir until cooked, approximately 2–3 minutes. Add salt and black pepper to taste.

Enjoy! (Preferably eaten with saltfish.)

**Important note:** Ackee that is picked from the tree must have ripened and split open on its own in order to be eaten; otherwise, it is poisonous. The red inner membrane and the big black seeds MUST be thrown away and NEVER eaten. Only the yellow flesh is edible. Canned ackee is recommended, as it has already been prepared safely for eating.

Servings: 4–6

# Saltfish

## Ingredients:
1/2 pound boneless salted codfish
1/2 cup vegetable oil
4 cloves garlic, chopped
2 onions, chopped
2 bell peppers (red, yellow, green, and/or orange), chopped
1 Scotch bonnet pepper, chopped (optional)
3 scallions, chopped
1 sprig thyme
1 teaspoon black pepper

## Directions:
Soak codfish in hot water for 1 hour. Replace water and soak codfish again in hot water for 1 more hour. (Codfish will soak for 2 hours total.) Heat oil in a large skillet or frying pan over medium-high heat and add garlic. Cook garlic for 20–30 seconds. Add onions, bell peppers, Scotch bonnet pepper, scallions, and thyme to the frying pan and stir occasionally until onions and peppers become translucent. Add codfish to sautéed vegetable mixture and stir for 5 minutes, until cooked. Sprinkle black pepper to taste.

Enjoy! (Preferably eaten with ackee and/or fried dumplings.)

Servings: 4–6

# Fried Plantains

## Ingredients:
4 plantains
1/4 cup vegetable oil
1 pinch salt

## Directions:
Peel the plantains and cut off the ends. Cut the plantains in half widthwise. Slice the plantains either lengthwise in strips or diagonally widthwise. Heat oil in a large skillet or frying pan over medium-high heat. Place the plantains into the hot oil and cook, turning occasionally, until tender and golden brown, approximately 3–5 minutes. Sprinkle a pinch of salt on top to taste if desired.

Enjoy and eat when cool!

Servings: 8–10

# FUN FACTS ABOUT JAMAICA

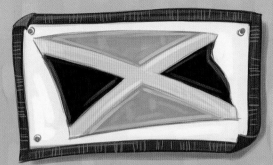

NATIONAL FLAG

NATIONAL MOTTO —
OUT OF MANY ONE PEOPLE

NATIONAL ANTHEM

NATIONAL DISH —
ACKEE AND SALTFISH

NATIONAL FLOWER —
LIGNUM VITAE

NATIONAL FRUIT —
ACKEE

CAPITAL CITY — KINGSTON

NATIONAL BIRD — DOCTOR BIRD